Dora's Fairy-tale Adventure

by Christine Ricci
based on a script by Eric Weiner
illustrated by Susan Hall

Published by Advance Publishers, L.C.
Maitland, FL 32751 USA
www.advancepublishers.com
Produced by Judy O Productions, Inc.
Designed by SunDried Penguin

Printed in China

ISBN 1-57973-310-7

Once upon a time . . . .

Dora and Boots were playing in Fairy-Tale Land.
Suddenly when Boots wasn't looking, a mean witch cast a spell and turned him into Sleeping Boots! The people of Fairy-Tale Land told Dora that the only thing that could wake Boots was a hug from a true princess.

Dora was worried. She didn't know any true princesses. "I have an idea!" exclaimed a friendly dwarf. "*You* can become a true princess and wake up Sleeping Boots."

The dwarfs told Dora that in order to become a true
princess she had to pass four tests. First she had to find
the red ring. Then she had to teach the giant rocks to sing.
Then she had to turn winter into spring. And finally she had
to bring the moon to the Queen and King.

Dora immediately set off to find the red ring. But it was hidden in a dark and scary cave. Dora didn't want to wake the Dragon who lived in the cave, so she quietly tiptoed inside. There she spotted the glow of the red ring.

But just as Dora reached for the ring, the Dragon awoke!

Dora quickly slipped the ring onto her finger. In a flash the Dragon's cave turned into a beautiful palace. And the mean dragon was transformed into a prince!

The Prince told Dora that the Mean Witch had turned him into a dragon. He was so grateful to Dora for setting him free that he gave Dora a magic music box.

"This will help you become a true princess," said the Prince.

Dora thanked him and started down the path toward her next test.

Soon Dora came upon the Giant Rocks.
"How can I teach these Giant Rocks to sing?" she wondered.
Then Dora remembered the magic music box that the Prince
had given her. She carefully turned the handle.

The music box started to play the most wonderful tune. The music was so delightful that Dora was sure it would make anyone sing and dance.

"Boingy, boingy, boingy, bing. We'll get these rocks to sing!" sang the magic music box.

Slowly the Giant Rocks opened their eyes. And then, to Dora's amazement, they began to dance and sing!
"*Boingy, boingy, boingy, bing. You've taught us how to sing!*"

When the song was over, Dora told the rocks that she had to be on her way.

"Sleeping Boots needs my help!" she said.

"Wait!" exclaimed the Giant Rocks as they gave Dora a present. "Here's a little bag of sunshine to help you become a true princess."

Dora thanked the Giant Rocks and ran down the path.

Soon Dora started to feel cold. Snow began to fall and a chilly wind whirled all around her.

"I must be in Winter Valley," she thought. "How will I turn winter into spring?"

Suddenly she remembered the little bag of sunshine. Dora opened the bag, and a small sun floated up into the sky.

The sun's rays melted all the snow. Flowers bloomed. Leaves grew on the trees. Birds, butterflies, and animals came out to play in the soft new grass.

"Thanks for turning winter into spring," said the animals.

"Take this magic hairbrush," said a little rabbit. "It will help you become a true princess so you can wake up Sleeping Boots."

At last Dora came upon a castle. She climbed the stairs to the top of a high tower. Now Dora faced the hardest test of all.

"How am I going to bring the moon to the Queen and King?" she wondered.

Dora looked up at the moon and knew that she was going to need some help from her friends.

Isa, Tico, and Benny heard Dora's call for help. But before they could reach her, the Mean Witch made the stairs to the tower disappear. Then Dora had a wonderful idea. She took out the magic hairbrush and began to brush her hair. With each stroke her hair grew longer until it hung all the way down to the ground.

Dora called down to her friends. "Come on! Climb up my hair!"

Dora asked Isa, Tico, and Benny to help her figure out a way to get to the moon. The friends thought hard, and soon they had a plan: They called to the stars!

The stars twinkled and glowed as they flew down from the sky. Then they made a staircase that led all the way to the moon!

Dora climbed and climbed
until she reached the moon.
"*¡Hola*, Dora!" said the moon.
"How can I help you?"
"Moon," said Dora, "I need you to visit
the Queen and King."
When the moon heard about Sleeping
Boots, he agreed to help her and floated
down to the tower.

"Dora," said the King. "You have found the red ring. You have taught the Giant Rocks to sing. You have turned winter into spring. And you have brought the moon to the Queen and King. You are now a true princess!"

The moon glowed in the sky. The stars twinkled. And rainbows danced through the air as Dora magically turned into a true princess!

"Hooray for Princess Dora!" everyone cheered.

The King's unicorns flew Princess Dora all the way back to Sleeping Boots.

Princess Dora wrapped her arms around Sleeping Boots and gave him the biggest hug ever! And then . . . Sleeping Boots opened his eyes!

And so Sleeping Boots awoke at last. The Mean Witch flew far, far away and was never seen again. And everyone in Fairy-Tale Land lived happily ever after!

The End